NICKELODEON

THE BIG
GREEN HELP™

Save the Tree!

adapted by Kermit Frazier
illustrated by Amy Marie Stadelmann, Little Airplane Productions

SIMON SPOTLIGHT/NICKELODEON
New York   London   Toronto   Sydney

Based on the TV series *Wonder Pets!*™ as seen on Nick Jr.®

SIMON SPOTLIGHT

An imprint of Simon & Schuster Children's Publishing Division
1230 Avenue of the Americas, New York, New York 10020
© 2009 Viacom International Inc. All rights reserved.
NICK JR., *Wonder Pets!*, and all related titles, logos, and characters are trademarks of Viacom International Inc. Nickelodeon,
The Big Green Help, and all related titles, logos, and characters are trademarks of Viacom International Inc.
All rights reserved, including the right of reproduction in whole or in part in any form.
SIMON SPOTLIGHT and colophon are registered trademarks of Simon & Schuster, Inc. Little Green Books and associated colophon
are trademarks of Simon & Schuster, Inc.
Manufactured in the United States of America
 10 9 8 7 6 5 4 3 2
ISBN-13: 978-1-4169-5111-7
ISBN-10: 1-4169-5111-3

Linny, Tuck, and Ming-Ming were in their cages, munching on some celery. Suddenly the tin-can phone began to ring!

The Wonder Pets put on their hats and rushed to answer the phone as they sang:

The phone! The phone is ringing!
The phone! We'll be right there!
There's an animal in trouble somewhere!

Linny picked up the phone, but she couldn't hear anything.

"Maybe it's a wrong number," said Ming-Ming Duckling.

"Look!" said Linny. "It's a little tree."

"It's all by itself in a dirty lot!" said Turtle Tuck.

"Do the Wonder Pets save trees?" asked Ming-Ming.

"Of course we do. Trees are living things, and we help all living things," said Linny. "We have to help the little tree!"

Linny, Tuck, and Ming-Ming changed into their hero outfits and started building the Flyboat so they could fly to the little tree's city.

"I can build the Flyboat by myself," said Ming-Ming, but the flying disc was too heavy for her.

"Sometimes you have to ask for help, no matter who you are," said Linny.

"Okay. Will you please help me?" asked Ming-Ming.

"Sure!" said Tuck. Together, the Wonder Pets lifted the disc and built the Flyboat.

"We are coming to save you, Little Tree!" called Ming-Ming as the Flyboat soared through the sky.
The Wonder Pets sang:

Wonder Pets! Wonder Pets!
We're on our way
to help a little tree
and save the day!

The Wonder Pets arrived at the city lot. "There's the little tree!" said Tuck. The poor tree didn't look very good. It had only three small leaves on its branches. Dirty boxes and trash were piled all around it.

"Let's clean up the lot so the little tree can get some sunlight," said Linny.

The Wonder Pets worked together to pick up all the trash in the lot. At last, sunlight shone on the little tree and a brave little bud poked out of the top branch.

But then one of the tree's three leaves trembled and fell to the ground. There were only two leaves left!

"We've got to do more for this little tree, team!" said Linny. "But what?"

Ming-Ming spotted a bucket of water nearby. "Maybe the little tree needs to be watered!" she said.

Together, the Wonder Pets lifted the bucket and gave the little tree a drink of water.
"How are you feeling, Little Tree?" asked Linny.

One of the tree's last two leaves began to tremble.

"Please don't fall!" cried Tuck. But it was too late. The leaf fell to the ground. Now there was only one leaf left!

"This is serious!" said Ming-Ming.

Tuck had an idea. "Trees are living things like us; they shouldn't be alone. Let's make a garden for the little tree so he won't be lonely."

"That's a great idea," said Linny, "but we can't plant a whole garden by ourselves."

"Sometimes you have to ask for help, no matter who you are," said
Ming-Ming.

The Wonder Pets asked the animals in the city to help them.
The city birds, squirrels, cats, and dogs helped the Wonder Pets
plant a beautiful garden for the little tree.

As the Wonder Pets and their animal friends worked, they sang:
What's going to work? Teamwork!
What's going to work? Teamwork!

At last the city garden was finished! The Wonder Pets and animals rushed over to the little tree. Its last leaf trembled. It looked like the last leaf was going to fall!

Then . . . *pop!* A beautiful flower blossomed on the happy little tree.

"We did it!" cried Tuck.

"It was a teamwork extravaganza!" said Ming-Ming.

"This calls for some celery!" said Linny.

The Wonder Pets sat under the little tree and shared fresh garden celery with their new city friends.